STUART·LITTLE ™

Stuart Finds His Way Home

Based on the screenplay by
Gregory J. Brooker and M. Night Shyamalan

HarperTrophy®
A Division of HarperCollins*Publishers*

COLUMBIA PICTURES PRESENTS A DOUGLAS WICK AND FRANKLIN/WATERMAN PRODUCTION A FILM BY ROB MINKOFF GEENA DAVIS 'STUART LITTLE' HUGH LAURIE AND JONATHAN LIPNICKI
CO-PRODUCER JASON CLARK MUSIC BY ALAN SILVESTRI EXECUTIVE PRODUCERS JEFF FRANKLIN AND STEVE WATERMAN BASED ON THE BOOK BY E.B. WHITE SCREENPLAY BY GREGORY J. BROOKER AND M. NIGHT SHYAMALAN
PRODUCED BY DOUGLAS WICK DIRECTED BY ROB MINKOFF DISTRIBUTED THROUGH SONY PICTURES RELEASING IN CANADA. DISTRIBUTED THROUGH COLUMBIA-TRISTAR FILMS OF CANADA

www.stuartlittle.com

COLUMBIA PICTURES

Stuart Little lived in a house in the city.
It wasn't a very big house,
but it was a special house.
Every Little in the world knew
how to find it.

Stuart's mother was named Mrs. Little.
His father was named Mr. Little.
His brother was named George.
And his cat was named Snowbell.

Snowbell did not like Stuart.
Although Stuart was a mouse,
he was a Little.
And Snowbell was not allowed to eat him.
All the neighborhood cats thought that was
funny.

Snowbell did not like to be laughed at.
So he decided to get rid of Stuart once and
for all.

One night he and some other cats
tricked Stuart into leaving.
Stuart went far away.
But he realized that he missed his family.
He wanted to go home.

The only way home was through the park.
The park was big and dark and scary.
But Stuart hopped into his car.
He raced through the park
as fast as he could.

Then he came to a fork in the road.
Which way should he go?
Stuart got out of his car to take a look.
All of a sudden he was surrounded by cats!

Stuart had to think fast.
He got into his car.
He stepped on the gas.
But the car went backward!
It skidded off the path
and flew down a hill.
The cats were still chasing Stuart.
So he turned the car around and
zoomed into a pipe!

The cats were getting closer.
One of them swiped at him
with its sharp claws.
Just in time, Stuart steered
out of harm's way.
Then he saw that the pipe was
coming to an end.
But there was no time to stop.
The car flew out of the pipe.

Splash! He landed in the water next to his ca
Stuart struggled to the surface
and climbed on top of his suitcase.
He was safe.
But wait! What was that sound?

He was headed straight for a waterfall!
Just as he was about to go over,
Stuart jumped up.
He landed on a grating
and held tight to the bars.

Wet and tired,
Stuart climbed up to the street.
How would he ever get home now?
But then he looked up.
He couldn't believe it—
he was staring right at his own house!

Stuart ran up the steps and tumbled
in through the mail slot.
But no one was home—except Snowbell.
Snowbell was not happy to see Stuart.

Not happy at all.
Snowbell did not tell Stuart
that the Littles had made posters
and were out looking for him.
"They're out celebrating," Snowbell lied.

The Littles were happy he was gone!
With nowhere else to go,
he ran back to the park, sobbing.
Stuart sat in a tree, thinking sad thoughts.
"Stuart!" he heard someone call.
It was Snowbell.
"What are you doing up there?" Snowbell
asked.
"Oh, just settling in," said Stuart.

Suddenly the mean cats appeared.
Stuart didn't seem too worried.
But Snowbell was frightened.
"Stuart, I lied!" yelled Snowbell.
He had just realized something.
Stuart was *his* family, too.
"Everyone misses you, Stuart! Please come
home!"

"Scratch
them
both!"
said one
of the cats.
"Yeeeehaaaa!" said Stuart, and he jumped.
He and Snowbell chased the cats away,
and together they walked home.

As they went in, George shouted with joy
and Mrs. Little cried.

Everyone was so happy to see Stuart!
They wanted to know how he had made it
back.

Stuart smiled a big smile.

"I couldn't have done it without Snowbell.
Besides, every Little in the world
can find the Little house!" he said.

Especially *Stuart* Little.